USBORNE FIRST READING

The Castle That Jack Built

Lesley Sims

Illustrated by Mike Gordon

Russell Punter

Illustrated by Peter Cottrill

Retold by Mairi Mackinnon

Illustrated by Mike and Carl Gordon

USBORNE FIRST READING

Chicken Licken

retold by Russell Punter

Illustrated by Ann Kronheimer

USBORNE FIRST READING

The Golden Goose

Retold by Conrad Mason

Illustrated by Mike and Carl Gordon

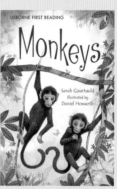

USBORNE FIRST READING

Monkeys

Sarah Courtauld

Illustrated by Daniel Howarth

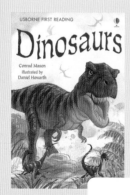

USBORNE FIRST READING

Dinosaurs

Conrad Mason

Illustrated by Daniel Howarth

USBORNE FIRST READING

The Magic Pear Tree

Retold by Rosie Dickins

Illustrated by Mabli Ward

USBORNE FIRST READING

The Magic Porridge Pot

Based on the story by The Brothers Grimm
Gordon

Tom Thumb

Retold by Katie Daynes
Illustrated by Wesley Robins

Reading consultant: Alison Kelly

This story is about

Thomas,

his wife Eve,

Merlin the
magician,

a crow,

King Arthur,

a fish

and, of course,
Tom Thumb.

Thomas really, really
wanted a son.

Even if he's no bigger
than a thumb.

So did his wife Eve.

"I'll go and see Merlin the magician," said Eve.

5

Sure enough, Eve had a
teeny tiny baby boy.

He was no bigger than
a thumb.

Eve made
little Tom a
cobweb top...

a pair of
woolly
shorts...

apple skin
shoes...

...and an
oak leaf hat.

He was healthy and happy,

but he never grew any
bigger.

One morning, Eve made some buns to sell at the market.

She couldn't find Tom anywhere, so she went to the market without him.

A tall man bought a bun.

He broke it open to eat...

...and got the shock of
his life.

Eve gasped. She washed
Tom and gave him a kiss.

The next day, she took
Tom to milk the cows.

She perched him on a
thistle to keep him safe...

...but cows like thistles.

"Tom, where are you?"
cried his mother.

She couldn't see him
anywhere.

Then a cow burped and
Tom tumbled out.

Eve washed her son and
gave him a kiss.

A week later, Tom went to sow seeds with his father.

"You can be the scarecrow," said Thomas. "Stand up and wave your arms."

The crows weren't scared
of little Tom Thumb.

One crow swooped down
and carried Tom away.

Tom wriggled and jiggled.

He jiggled so much, the crow dropped him.

Down and down he fell...

SPLOSH!

...into the lake.

Little Tom was swallowed
by a fish.

The fish was caught by
a fisherman.

That evening, the fish was
served to King Arthur.

The King got the shock of
his life.

...and so did the Queen
and the princesses.

I always win at
hide-and-seek.

Even the big, bold knights liked Tom Thumb.

I can slay a dragon with one swipe of my sword.

"I shall make you a knight
too," said the King.

"You must have new
clothes, and your
own horse."

Brave Sir Tom hunted
down spiders...

...and chased after
dragonflies.

He collected falling
petals and rescued
drowning moths.

The King invited Tom to
stay forever.

"I'd like that very much," said Tom. "But first I must go home."

My mother will be worried.

"Of course," said the King. "And you must take a gift from me."

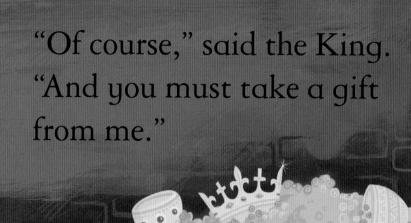

He showed Tom his treasure room.

Tom set off home with a shiny gold coin.

"Tom!" called Eve.

"Is it really you?"
cried Thomas.

"Yes, it's me!" replied Tom.
"I'm Sir Tom now."

Tom told his parents all
about his adventures.

"I'm the King's chief pea
juggler," he said.

In the morning, Tom
headed back to the castle.

"Be careful, Tom," his
mother called out.

"Don't worry, I'll be
fine," he replied...
and he was.

Designed by Sam Whibley
Series designer: Russell Punter
Series editor: Lesley Sims

First published in 2014 by Usborne Publishing Ltd.,
Usborne House, 83-85 Saffron Hill, London EC1N 8RT, England.
www.usborne.com Copyright © 2014 Usborne Publishing Ltd.

USBORNE FIRST READING
Level Four

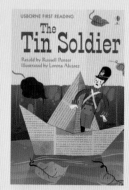

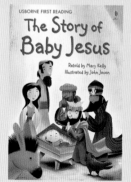

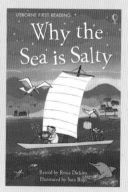

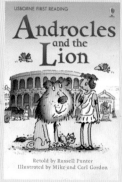

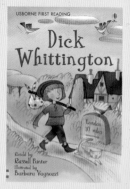